Whiffy Wilson

The Wolf who wouldn't go to school

Caryl Hart   **Leonie Lord**

ORCHARD

Whiffy Wilson

the wolf who wouldn't go to school

For the children of Meridian Primary School, Peacehaven.
Well done with your fantastic reading. Keep it up! – C.H

To Molly and Jack – L.L

ORCHARD BOOKS
338 Euston Road, London NW1 3BH
Orchard Books Australia
Level 17/207 Kent Street, Sydney, NSW 2000

First published in 2014 by Orchard Books

ISBN 978 1 40835 600 5

Text © Caryl Hart 2014
Illustrations © Leonie Lord 2014
The rights of Caryl Hart to be identified as the author and of Leonie Lord to be
identified as the illustrator of this book have been asserted by them in accordance
with the Copyright, Designs and Patents Act, 1988.

A CIP catalogue record for this book is available from the British Library.

1 3 5 7 9 10 8 6 4 2

Printed in China

Orchard Books is a division of Hachette Children's Books, an Hachette UK company.
www.hachette.co.uk

There was a wolf called Wilson
Who couldn't count to ten.
He wouldn't learn to write his name.
He never used a pen.

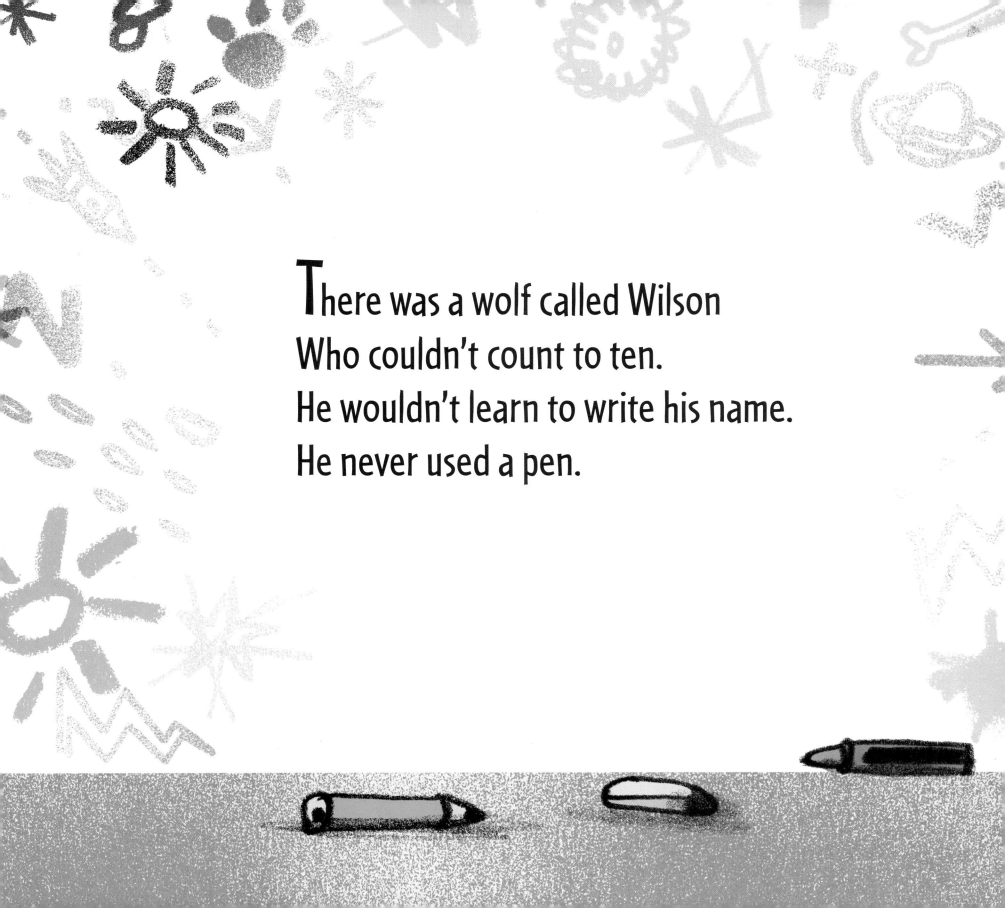

He didn't know his A B Cs.

He couldn't paint or cook.

He wouldn't learn his two-plus-twos.

He never read a book.

"Time for School!"

his father cried,

"You pesky little pup!"

"But school is **BORING!**" Wilson whined,
And he turned the telly up.

One morning, Wilson went next door
To ask his friend to play.
But Dotty smiled, "I can't because
I'm off to school today."

"Well, *I'm* not going," Wilson grumped.
"Who wants to read and write?
I'd rather play and watch TV
And stay up late at night."

"Oh, you're so silly," Dotty smiled.
"Come to school with me!
There's nothing to be scared of –
School's lots of fun, you'll see!"

"WHO SAYS I'M SCARED?"
growled Wilson.
"A wolf is brave and strong.
It's just ... the teacher might be cross
If I get the answers wrong."

But Dotty wasn't worried,
She just grabbed him by the paw.
She marched him up the path to school
And pushed him through the door.

She hung his coat up on a peg,
She made him use the loo,
Then took him to the classroom
And showed him what to do.

"First you paint a picture
And stick it on the wall."

"Then you get some biscuit dough
And roll it in a ball.
You squeeze it and you squash it
And you pat it nice and flat,

Then get some biscuit cutters
And make a shape – like that!"

"Next you get the ladybirds
And count up all the spots.
Then we'll draw a picture
By joining up these dots."

At lunchtime they had pizza.
Then ran to play outside.
"Let's play football!" called a boy.
"My favourite!" Wilson cried.

He ran and passed and dribbled,
Then he scored a goal – hooray!
His team cheered, **"Whiffy Wilson,**
You're the Hero of the Day!"

"I thought no one would like me,"
Said Wilson with a grin.
"But look at all my lovely friends.
It's great fun joining in."

In Messy Time that afternoon
They made a flying car.
"What lovely work," the teacher smiled.
"You've earned a golden star."

Dotty

Wilson

"This isn't work!" gasped Wilson.
"All we've done so far is play!"
"Oh, you're so funny," Dotty laughed.
"We've been working hard all day!"

But the day was nearly over
So they sat down on the rug.
The teacher read a story
And Wilson gave his friend a hug.

"This school is perfect," Wilson grinned,
"It isn't dull at all.
I can play with all the other kids.
I can run, and kick a ball!"

"The classroom toys are really cool.
The teacher is so kind.
If I had to come here every day,
I really wouldn't mind!"

Next morning, Whiffy Wilson
Was up and dressed at eight.
He called for Dotty straightaway,
"It's school – we can't be late!"

"Oh, Whiffy Wilson," Dotty smiled.
"You really are the best!
There's no school on a *Saturday* –
It's time to have a rest!"

"But home is BORING!" Wilson whined.
"I want to go and play.
What can I do? Just stay inside
And watch TV all day?"

"Never mind," smiled Dotty.
"You can come and play with me."

So they ran around the garden,
As happy as can be.

the End.